Tell Me One Good Thing
Bedtime Stories

by Richard Thompson
art by Eugenie Fernandes

Annick Press • Toronto

Annick Press Ltd.

Annick Press gratefully acknowledges the support of the
Canadian Council and the Ontario Arts Council.

Canadian Cataloguing in Publication Data

Thompson, Richard, 1951 —
    Tell me one good thing

ISBN 1-55037-215-7 (bound) ISBN 1-55037-212-2 (pbk.)

I. Fernandes, Eugenie, 1943 -   . II. Title.

PS8589.H65T4   1992   jC813′.54   C91-094804-6
PZ7.T56Te   1992

The art in this book was rendered in watercolours,
coloured pencils, crayon and other media. The text has
been set in various styles by Attic Typesetting Inc.

Distributed in Canada and the USA by:
Firefly Books Ltd.
250 Sparks Avenue
Willowdale, Ontario   M2H 2S4

Printed and bound in Hong Kong.

CONTENTS

Tell Me One Good Thing

Tell me one good thing
            about yourself,
One thing you truly treasure.

Tell me one good thing
            about today,
One thing that gave you pleasure.

Tell me one good thing
            about tomorrow,
One thing you hope to do.

Tell me one good thing
            you'll think about
As sleep comes softly to you.

Let good things fill
            your dreams tonight
With happy thoughts and
            laughing ones.

Keep warm, my child.
            Sleep tight, my love
Until the morning comes.

SNOW BEAR

Annie and her mother stood with their noses on the cold glass, watching the first fat flakes of the first snow of winter dancing quiet as dreams through the dark sky.

When the ten billionth snowflake settled on the back walk, Annie's mom said softly, "Time for bed, my girl."

When her mother had kissed her and gone downstairs, Annie took all her blankets and piled them into a mountain on her bed. She dug a cave in the middle of the mountain. She was just about to crawl into the cave when her mother poked her head into the room.

"Annie, what are you doing? You're supposed to go to sleep."

"I'm not going to sleep, Mom," said Annie. "I'm hibernating. This is my cave."

"Ah," said her mother, "hibernating . . . well, have a good hibernate. We'll see you in the spring time."

Annie crawled deep into the cave. It was dark and warm. Deeper still she crawled, until— BOOMP! What was that? Something big. Something furry. Something rumbling, soft and low.

"Mama Bear, is that you?" whispered Annie. "It's me—Annie."

"Hrmph," grunted Mama Bear. "Time for you to sleep, little cub."

Annie rested her head against Mama Bear's belly. Mama Bear put her arm around her little cub and rumbled back to sleep.

But Annie couldn't sleep. She wasn't used to being in a cave. It was awfully quiet and awfully dark.

"Mama Bear," she whispered. "Mama Bear, I can't go to sleep."

Mama Bear stirred. "What is it, Annie? What's the matter?"

"I can't sleep, Mama Bear. Tell me some good things to think about, so I can sleep."

"Well, little one," said Mama Bear, "when I was a cub and couldn't sleep, I would always think of snow. I would think of snow falling softly, snow blowing and swirling. I would think about snow wet on my nose, and snow tingly on my tongue. I would think of the world wrapped in white, bright in the day and woolly at night. I would think about sliding and rolling and jumping in snow. And best of all, I would think about building a snow bear—as big as a blizzard. And then I could sleep. But we bears hibernate till spring time, so, of course, by the time I woke up the snow was all gone. But I dreamed cool, and fluffy snow-covered dreams. Annie . . . Annie?"

Annie was asleep. She dreamed of snow, swirling and tingly, woolly and bright.

When it was spring time in her dreams, she woke up and stretched and yawned.

Mama Bear was still rumbling in her sleep, so very, very quietly Annie crawled out of the cave into the morning of her room.

"Good morning, Annie," smiled her mother. "Did you have a good sleep?"

"Is it spring time?" Annie asked.

"Oh, no," said her mother. "It's just the start of winter."

"I'm glad," said Annie, "I want to jump and slide and roll in the snow and make a snow bear as big as a blizzard."

And right after breakfast, she did.

Rock-A-Bye

Rock-a-bye, baby, in the tree top . . .
Hey! That's not a good place to be.
Rock-a-bye, baby, but
Rock-a-bye, baby,
Snuggled up warm here with me.

And when the wind blows,
Don't worry at all;
I'll hold you real tight,
I won't let you fall.

So, rock-a-bye, baby, safe in your bed,
Rock-a-bye, baby, sweet dreams in your head.

Wind-Blow and Bough-Break won't bother you.

Rock-a-bye, Rock-a-bye,
all the night through.

Way Below
Above Her Head

Jesse liked it when her dad threw her in the air and caught her. But one time, he threw her too high, and she went tumbling end over end over end, up and up and up and up . . . until she felt her feet touch something cool and smooth. She bounced a couple of times and stopped.

She looked around. Away above her head, far below her, she could see her dad waving his arms. He seemed to be shouting, but she couldn't hear his words.

All the trees and all the buildings and the people and the cars were hanging upside down above her head, and she . . . she was standing on the sky.

She tried to walk. The sky was springy under her feet and felt very good. She tried to run. The sky was smooth and empty, and she could run like the wind. She ran for a long time, and then sat down cross-legged on the sky and watched the things *above* her head.

A jet plane roared by, way below, above her head. The noise of its engines made the sky shake like jelly in a bowl.

A helicopter chattered through the air, way below, above her head.

She saw the fat round top of a hot air balloon floating by, way below, above her head.

A glider swept silently above her, far below.

A bird came and landed upside-down on her hand and then flew away again.

The sun came *creeping* slowly across the sky. Jesse began to feel sleepy. Her eyes kept trying to close. But she didn't want to go to sleep. She was worried that, if she fell asleep, she might fall off the sky and tumble up to the ground. So she stood up to move away from the sun, where it would be a little bit cooler.

As she stood up something brushed against her head. Jesse cried out and swatted at the thing that was attacking her. When she realised that it was only a brightly colored kite, it was too late. She had already ripped it, so that it couldn't fly anymore. She watched it flutter helplessly up toward the ground.

"I'm sorry!" she called after it.

She walked a long way to get away from the hot, hot sun. When it was cool enough, she sat down again and looked up. Above, between her and the ground, and between her and her mom and dad, a quilt of clouds stretched forever in all directions.

Jesse suddenly realized that she had come a long way from home. She felt lonely and a little afraid. She thought about crying, but, instead, she stood up and started walking across the sky following the sun.

Eventually, the one huge cloud below, above her head, began to break into a lot of little clouds. A rainbow formed over and around her in a fizz of color. It wafted up into the clouds and floated into a graceful loop that reached up to the ground at both ends.

The sun sailed up toward the ground and disappeared behind the hanging circle of the Earth.

The stars came out. They looked like sharp splinters of glass. The stars covered the sky, and even walking on the top of her tiptoes, Jesse found herself stepping on some. But to her surprise, they tingled pleasantly against the bottoms of her feet.

Once in a while, one of the stars would break away and go streaking up to join the clusters of stars on the ground above, which were really the lights of fires and cars and trains and cities.

Far above, below her feet, spaceships winked and whirred. None stopped to offer her a ride, and she would have said, "No, thank you," if one had. She wanted to go home.

She walked and walked. All of a sudden, she felt very tired.

The moon came up behind her, spreading its cool light around the sky.

"I don't want to walk any more," Jesse said. "I will ride on the moon for a while."

She stepped onto the shiny moon. But the moon was very slippery and Jesse's feet flew out from under her. She tumbled end over end over end, up and up and up, down and down and down, until she landed with a soft plop on a sandy beach.

Two people were sitting side by side on the sand with their arms around each other, watching the sky.

"Mom! Dad!" Jesse called.

Her mom and dad came running and scooped her up in their arms and hugged her and kissed her and hugged her some more until the moon went down.

Dream Dance

Your pillow's the stage,
  The spotlight's the moon
The stars are all out
  To carry the tune.
Dance dream and dream dance,
  All quick the night long.
You are the dancer
  The watcher,
  The dance
  And the song.

PATIENT, PATIENT

"I still don't feel any better, doctor," said Jane's mom in a croaky whisper. "I don't think those pills work for sore throats."

The doctor looked at the bottle.

"You are right, patient," she said. "These pills are for red spots on your belly. Do you have red spots on your belly?"

Jane's mom looked under the covers. "No," she said, "No spots..."

"Hmmm...what can I do now?" said the doctor. "I know! I'll give you a shot!"

"I don't like shots," croaked Jane's mom.

"I know that shots hurt, but it's for just a minute and then it won't hurt anymore. There, that didn't hurt, did it?"

"No, it didn't hurt," said Jane's mom. "Thank you, doctor."

"Do you feel better, patient?"

"No," said Jane's mom.

"Well, medicine takes a little while to work," said the doctor. "You have to be patient. Hey! That's funny! You are my patient, and you have to be patient! Don't you think that's funny?"

The patient just groaned and pulled the covers up around her chin.

The doctor closed her bag.

"I am going to go and make you some soup," she said. "I won't be gone long. Be patient, patient."

"I will make healthy soup," said the doctor as she cut up some broccoli and threw it into a pot with water. She added some liver and onions and a big spoon full of cottage cheese. She smashed up a turnip and added that.

"I will put in all the things that are good for you," she said to herself. Then she added a can of spinach, a can of cream of asparagus soup, a whole fish with the head still on, and some lentils.

"Now it has to cook."

"Be patient, patient," she called. "The soup will be ready soon."

The doctor read a book and waited for the soup to cook.

"Just be patient, patient. It's cooking."

She coloured a picture and waited for the soup to cook.

"Just be patient, patient. It's almost done!"

And finally the soup was ready.

The doctor ladled some into a big bowl and took it to Jane's mom.

Jane's mom scooped a spoonful and moved it toward her open mouth, but the spoon stopped half-way there and wouldn't move any further.

"Doctor, this soup smells awful!"

"I know it smells awful," said the doctor, "but it's good for you. Take a bite."

"I can't do it, doctor. It's too horrible!" Jane's mom put the spoon down and crossed her arms.

"Would you like me to feed you?" asked the doctor.

Jane's mom closed her mouth tightly and shook her head.

With a big sigh, the doctor took away the soup.

"Well, I don't know what to do then," she said. "I tried hitting you on the knee with my hammer. I tried listening to your heart. I took your temperature and checked your blood."

"Maybe I need an operation," suggested Jane's mom.

"An operation? That's pretty serious. Let me do a test first."

The doctor picked up her eye-looking-in-thing and held it up to Jane's mom's eye. She looked for a long time.

"Let me look in your ears," she said. "This is bad. There's nothing in there. Your head is empty! No wonder you're sick! Wait here."

"Where are you going, doctor?" whispered Jane's mom.

"Just be patient, patient. I will be right back."

When the doctor came back she was carrying a whole pile of books.

"You have to read all of these books," she said. "We have to get your head filled back up again—fast."

"Could you read them to me?" croaked Jane's mom.

"Well, doctors don't usually read books to their patients..."

"Please."

"Well, alright," said the doctor, "but only because this is an emergency."

As Jane's mom lay back down on her pillow, the doctor took the first book from the top of the pile and started to read. By the time she had finished the third book the patient's eyes were closed and she was breathing softly. The doctor closed the book very quietly. She leaned over and gave the patient a kiss.

"Doctors don't usually kiss their patients," she whispered, "but this is an emergency."

Then she tiptoed out of the room.

A little while later Jane's mom woke up.

"Doctor!" she called. "Doctor, I feel much better."

The doctor smiled and checked her eyes and ears again.

"It still seems pretty dark and empty in there," she said. "But keep reading, and it will fill up in time. Just be patient, patient. Would you like some soup now?"

"No, thank you," said Jane's mom. "I feel much better actually. I think I will get up now. Pass me my slippers, please."

"Well," said the doctor, "doctors don't usually pass slippers, but if you're sure you're better..."

"Oh, I am! I am!"

"I can stop being the doctor, and I can be your little girl again."

"Jane," said Jane's mom, "you are a wonderful doctor. And a wonderful daughter!"

Chilliwack

The spaceship had orange and blue blinking lights, and it made a funny beeping noise—bedoop, bedoop, bedoop! With his two quarters, Robbie could ride once in the spaceship. Or he could ride TWICE on the golden horse.

"I want to go on the horse, Dad," he said.

Robbie's dad lifted him onto the back of the shiny horse.

"I am going to Chilliwack," said Robbie.

Robbie's good friend, Jennie, had just moved away to Chilliwack and everyone in the family missed her very much.

"Give Jennie a hug for us," said his mom.

"I will," said Robbie. He dropped his quarter in the money slot. He held onto the reins and . . . nothing happened!

"Giddyap!" said Robbie. He shook the reins. "Go to Chilliwack!"

The horse turned his head and looked at Robbie with one big brown eye.

"Oh," he said. "PLEASE, giddyap!"

The horse set off aclattering through the shopping mall, dodging daintily amongst the busy shoppers. He stepped gingerly onto the automatic door opener, and when the door soushed open, he pranced into the sunlight, tossed his mane and galloped away across the parking lot.

He cantered across the city.
He jumped across the river.
He trotted through the meadows filled with flowers
and walked softly through dark forests.
Robbie patted his neck and said, "Good horsey!"

The horse galloped through a stony canyon and under a rainbow.

He swam across sparkling lakes with Robbie balanced on his back like a circus rider.

He raced beside a rumbling train and left it far behind.

He outran a bus and a truck full of sheep.

And then, quite suddenly, outside an ice cream store in a little town, the horse stopped.

"Giddyap!" said Robbie.

But the horse wouldn't.

"Please, giddyap!" said Robbie.

But the horse didn't.

"PLEASE, Please, Giddyap!" cried Robbie.

But the horse stood there as still as a statue.

A boy came out of the store balancing a triple scoop ice cream cone. He stopped licking for a moment and looked at Robbie and the horse.

"You have to put a quarter in," he said.

Of course! Robbie reached into his pocket and pulled out his other quarter. He put the quarter in the money slot.

"Please, go to Chilliwack," Robbie cried.

The horse bounded forward. But he'd only gone a bound and a leap when Robbie realized that he had no quarters left to take him home again.

"Wait!" he called. But the horse was so excited about going to Chilliwack, he didn't even hear Robbie.

He galloped through dark tunnels and by a rushing river.

He jumped over low clouds and medium-sized mountains.

Robbie held on tight. He wasn't sure if he was happy or scared, so he laughed, just in case.

With a great final leap, the horse landed beside a plum tree in a valley full of flowering plum trees.

Robbie knew he wasn't going to go on. He had no more quarters.

"I'm pretty close to Chilliwack," Robbie said to himself. "I think I can walk."

He started out, and in no time at all he came to those stairs that go up to Chilliwack. Up he went—up and up and up and up and up the stairs to Chilliwack.

Robbie knocked on the door of Jennie's house. Nobody answered. He rang the doorbell. Nobody answered. What if Jennie wasn't home? He rang the doorbell once more. Nobody answered.

Robbie sat down on the steps and felt very lonely. He had just about decided to start to cry when he heard a sound in the air, a funny beeping noise . . . bedoop, bedoop, bedoop! He looked up and saw orange and blue blinking lights. It was the spaceship from the shopping mall.

The spaceship landed on the lawn. Robbie's dad was driving and Robbie's mom was riding in the back. They both jumped out, ran over and gave Robbie a great big hug.

At that moment, Jennie and *her* mom and dad came home. Everybody hugged everybody—twice. Then the big people sat in the kitchen and talked while Robbie and Jennie laughed and played and sang songs and talked and laughed some more.

Finally, it was time to go home.

"We'll come and visit again," said Robbie's mom when she saw Jennie's sad face. "On the way back, you can ride with me in the spaceship, Robbie, Daddy will ride the horse. Okay?"

"Okay," said Robbie.

Out in the yard, everybody hugged everybody once again. Then, under a fat Chilliwack moon, Robbie and his mom got into the spaceship. Robbie put some quarters into the money slot. The spaceship began to rise up into the sky—bedoop, bedoop, bedoop!

Robbie looked over the side of the spaceship. Jennie looked very, very tiny way down on the ground. Robbie blew her a kiss. Jennie blew one back to him.

"Goodbye, Robbie," called Jennie.

"Goodbye, Jennie!"

"Goodbye, Chilliwack."

The spaceship flew away into the night. Robbie snuggled into his mom's arms, closed his eyes, and slept all the way home.

A House

Dig holes in the dark.
    Fill them with laughter.

Tie moonbeam to moonbeam
    For wall and for rafter.

Cover with breezes
    Scented with flowers,

Fasten in place
    With minutes and hours.

Make windows from star light,
    The door from a song.

As big as you want it,
    and butterfly strong.

Worries

Aunt Sandy brought them for Becky from a country far, far away—four tiny dolls who lived in a tiny cloth bag.

"They're worry dolls, Becky," Aunt Sandy told her. "When you go to bed at night you can tell your worries to the dolls. Keep them under your pillow, and you will have happy dreams."

Becky did what Aunt Sandy said to do. Each night she whispered to the dolls:

"Rosa, I am worried that I will fall and hurt myself if Daddy takes the training wheels off my bike."

"Maria, I am worried about walking past Mrs. Johnson's house because her dog may bite me."

"Teresa, I am worried about PIGGY IN A PUDDLE. It's a library book, and I don't know where it is."

"Juanita, I am worried about the dentist; Aleisha says it hurts."

And every night she had happy dreams.

But one night she thought of a worry she hadn't

thought of before.

"Rosa, I am worried," she whispered. "Do my worries make you worried? Do my worries give *you* bad dreams?"

That night Becky awoke in the dark. A tiny voice was calling her name.

"Becky! Becky! Wake up! It is me—Rosa. Do not be frightened."

Becky switched on her lamp. Standing on her quilt were the four little dolls—Rosa and Maria, Teresa and Juanita.

"You were worried about the worries that you give to us each night," said Maria.

"We have come to show what we can do with your worries, so you won't worry about that any more," said Teresa. "Sometimes Rosa takes your worries and makes them into songs."

Becky listened as Rosa sang in her small, sweet voice a song in a language that Becky did not know.

"And sometimes," said Juanita, "Maria takes your worries and makes them into dances."

Becky watched Maria twirl and leap across the patterns of her quilt.

"That was beautiful," she said when Maria finished her dance. "What do you do, Teresa?"

"Ah," said Teresa. "Sometimes I take your worries and I spin them into fine yarn for weaving. See . . ."

She showed Becky a spool of brightly coloured thread.

"And I weave the thread," said Juanita. She showed Becky her tiny loom.

"Will you make a dress out of the cloth?" asked Becky.

"Not a dress," said Juanita.

"What then?"

"I will tell you," said the doll, "but you must promise that you will not worry."

"I promise," said Becky.

"When the cloth is big enough," said Juanita, "we will fly away on it. We will go far, far away."

"Back to your country?" asked Becky.

"Yes."

"But what about my worries?" Becky sounded worried.

"Your mother or your father will listen," said Rosa.

"But . . ."

"You promised not to worry," Maria reminded her. "We will not go soon."

For many more nights Becky gave her worries to the dolls for singing, dancing, spinning and weaving. She forgot to worry about the flying cloth.

One night she couldn't find her dolls. She looked under her bed and in the cupboard, in her toy box and amongst her books. But the dolls were gone.

"I am worried about my dolls," she told her mom that night. "I can't find them anywhere."

Becky's mother sang to her. She wove her fingers amongst the fine threads of Becky's hair and let them dance gently across her cheek.

Becky slept, and in her dreams she saw Rosa and Maria, Teresa and Juanita laughing and singing as they floated through the sky to a country far, far away.

Always Summer

It's freezing hot on Jupiter
And colder in James Bay.
Monsoons hit Manitoba
But I say, "That's okay..."

Because...
Whether the weather is foul or fine,
I'm toasty warm in this bed of mine.

There's sleet and snow in Toronto
It's hailing in Quebec.
There's a blizzard in the bird cage,
But I say, "What the heck!"

Because...
Whether the weather brings sun or storm
Under my covers I'm snuggly warm.

A hurricane in the kitchen
And thunder in the hall.
A dust storm in the closet—they
Don't bother me at all.

Because...
Whether the weather whistles or screams,
It's always summer here in my dreams.

Lullaby Lost

"Isn't Mommy going to sing to me tonight?" asked Emily sadly.

"I'm sorry," said her dad. "Your mommy's lost her voice. She can't talk at all."

"Where did she lose it?" asked Emily. "Will she find it again?"

"She'll find it again," said her dad. "She'll be able to sing to you again soon. Goodnight, Emily. I love you."

"I love you, too."

That night, Emily heard singing in the dark outside her window. It was the song her mother sang for her every night at bedtime:

"Hush, little baby, don't say a word,
Mommy's gonna buy you a mocking
bird . . ."

"It's mommy's lost voice!" Emily whispered. "I have to get it and bring it back."

She crept out into the yard, past the sandbox, past the garden shed. The singing was coming from a box in the corner by the fence. Emily crept closer, ready to grab the voice and take it back to her mom.

But when she looked into the box she saw . . . a mommy cat singing to her kittens.

"And if that mockingbird don't sing,
Mama's gonna buy you a diamond
ring . . ."

It was her mother's song, but it wasn't her mother's voice.

The kittens closed their tiny eyes. The mommy cat stopped singing and closed hers too.

As she walked back to the house, Emily heard the voice again:

"And if that diamond ring turns brass,
Mama's gonna buy you a looking glass..."

...but now it seemed to be coming from the tree in Mr. Gibbin's yard.

"Aha!" thought Emily. Over the fence and up the tree she went. High in the branches of the tree she discovered...a mother bird, singing to her babies:

"And if that looking glass gets broke,
Mama's gonna buy you a billy goat..."

It was her mother's song, but it wasn't her mother's voice.

But when the mother bird stopped singing and tucked her head under her wing, Emily could hear another voice sing. It was coming from far away where the moon shone on the river — too far away to hear the words.

Emily ran to the river, but it wasn't her mother's voice she found. All the mother fishes in the whole wide river were singing to their minnows, and the river was humming along:
"And if that billy goat won't pull,
Mommy's gonna buy you a cart and bull . . . *"*

It was her mother's song, but it wasn't her mother's voice.

Emily was getting very sleepy. She wanted to go home to bed, but she was too sleepy. She curled up in a ball by a huckleberry bush and closed her eyes.

The last thing she heard was a mother dragon singing to her baby in a cave nearby:
"And if that cart and bull tip over,
Mommy's gonna buy you a dog named Rover . . . *"*

Emily was already sound asleep when the dragon mother came out of her cave to stretch her wings and look at the stars.

The dragon mother was surprised to see Emily sleeping there by the huckleberry bush. She picked the girl up ever so gently in her long curved claws, spread her great green wings and soared across the night sky. As she soared, the dragon mother sang to Emily in her scaley voice:

"And if that Dog named Rover won't bark,
Mommy's gonna buy you a horse and
cart . . ."

Back they flew to Emily's waiting bed.

Cozy now, Emily dreamed that her mother's voice had come back home and was hiding in the cupboard in the bathroom.

When Emily woke, she ran into her mother's room.

"I know where it is, Mom! I know where it is!"

Her mother wasn't there.

Emily ran into the bathroom. There was her mother, combing her hair in front of the mirror. She must have looked in the cupboard, because she had found her voice and was singing:

"And if that horse and cart fall down,
You're still the sweetest little baby in
town . . ."

44

Sleep, Wee Worm

Sleep, wee worm
   in your warm cocoon.
The sun will come to kiss you soon,
To show you the wonder
   a new day brings,
And watch
as you spread your brand new wings.

From dreams that are gentle
   or dreams that are wild,
You will awaken, a different child,
A wee bit wiser,
   a tiny bit grown.
But I'll love you the same,
   my child, my own.

Other books by Richard Thompson:

Jenny's Neighbours

Foo

Gurgle Bubble Splash

Effie's Bath

Maggee and the Lake Minder

Sky Full of Babies

I Have to See This

Jesse on the Night Train

Zoe and the Mysterious X